The Leviathan

The Leviathan

·

JOSEPH ROTH

Translated by Michael Hofmann

A NEW DIRECTIONS PEARL

PUBLISHER'S NOTE
The Leviathan, in Michael Hofmann's translation, first appeared in *The Collected
Stories of Joseph Roth* and is published here by arrangement with W. W. Nor-
ton & Company

Manufactured in the United States of America
New Directions Books are printed on acid-free paper.
First published as a Pearl (NDP1207) by New Directions in 2011
Published simultaneously in Canada by Penguin Books Canada Limited
Design by Erik Rieselbach

Library of Congress Cataloging-in-Publication Data

Roth, Joseph, 1894–1939.
[Leviathan. English]
The leviathan / Joseph Roth ; translated by Michael Hofmann.
    p. cm.
"A New Directions Pearl."
ISBN 978-0-8112-1925-9 (pbk. : acid-free paper) — ISBN 978-0-8112-1932-7
(ebook)
I. Hofmann, Michael, 1957 Aug. 25– II. Title.
PT2635.O84L4213 2011
833'.912—dc22   2011007595

10 9 8 7 6 5 4 3 2 1

New Directions Books are published for James Laughlin
by New Directions Publishing Corporation
80 Eighth Avenue, New York, NY 10011

Contents

THE LEVIATHAN

I

IN THE SMALL town of Progrody there lived a coral merchant who was known far and wide for his honesty and the reliability and quality of his wares. The farmers' wives came to him from far-distant villages when they needed an ornament for some festive occasion. There were other coral merchants who were closer at hand, but they knew that from them they would only get cheap stuff and no-good tat. And so, in their rickety little carts they traveled many versts to Progrody and the renowned coral merchant, Nissen Piczenik.

They tended to come on market days, which were Mondays and Thursdays for horses and pigs respectively. While their menfolk were busy sizing up the animals, the women would go off together in little groups, barefooted, their boots dangling over their shoulders, with their brightly colored scarves that shone even on rainy days, to the house of Nissen Piczenik. The tough bare soles of their feet pattered happily along the hollow-planked wooden pavement, and down the broad cool passage of the old building where the merchant lived. The arching passageway led into a quiet yard where soft moss sprouted among the uneven cobblestones, and the occasional blade of grass raised its head in summer. Here Nissen Piczenik's flock of chickens came joyfully out to meet them, the cocks leading the way with their proud red combs as red as the reddest of the corals.

They would knock three times on the iron door with the iron knocker. At that, Piczenik would open a little grille cut into the door, see who was outside, and draw the bolt and allow the farmers' wives to come in. In the case of beggars, traveling musicians, gypsies, and men with dancing bears, he would merely pass a coin out through the grille. He had to be very careful because on each of the tables in his large kitchen and his parlor he had fine corals in large, small, and middle-sized heaps, various races and breeds of corals all mixed up, or already sorted according to color and type. He didn't have so many eyes in his head that he could see what every beggar was up to, and Piczenik knew how seductively poverty led to sin. Of course, some prosperous farmers' wives sometimes stole things, too; for women are always tempted to help themselves illicitly and clandestinely to an item of jewelry they can comfortably afford to buy. But where his customers were concerned, the merchant would tend to turn a blind eye, and he included a few thefts in the prices he charged for his wares anyway.

He employed no fewer than ten threaders, pretty girls with keen eyes and soft hands. The girls sat in two rows either side of a long table, and fished for the corals with their fine needles. They put together beautiful regular necklaces, with the smallest corals at either end, and the largest and most brilliant in the middle. As they worked, the girls sang. On the hot, blue, sunny days of summer, when the long table where the women sat threading was set up outside in the yard, you could hear their summery voices all over the little town, louder than the twittering skylarks and the chirruping of the crickets in the gardens.

Most people, who only know corals from seeing them in shop windows and displays, would be surprised to learn how many different varieties of them there are. For a start, they can be polished or not; they can be trimmed in a straight line or rounded off; there are thorny and stick-like corals that look like barbed wire; corals that gleam with a yellowish, almost a whitishred, like the rims of tea-rose petals; pinkish-yellow, pink, brick red, beet red, cinnabar red corals; and finally there are those corals that look like hard, round drops of blood. There are rounds and half-rounds; corals like little barrels and little cylinders; there are straight, crooked, and even hunchbacked corals. They come as stars, spears, hooks, and blossoms. For corals are the noblest plants in the oceanic underworld; they are like roses for the capricious goddesses of the sea, as inexhaustible in their variety as the caprices of the goddesses.

As you see, then, Nissen Piczenik didn't have a shop as such. He ran his business from home, which meant that he lived among the corals night and day, summer and winter, and as all the windows in his parlor and kitchen opened onto the courtyard and were protected by thick iron bars, there was in his apartment a beautiful and mysterious twilight that was like the light under the sea, and it was as though corals were not merely traded here, but that this was where they actually grew. Furthermore, thanks to a strange and canny quirk of nature, the coral merchant Nissen Piczenik was a red-haired Jew with a copper-colored goatee that looked like a particular kind of reddish seaweed, which gave the man a striking resemblance to a sea god. It was as though he made his corals himself, or maybe sowed and reaped them in some way. In fact, so strong was the association between his wares and his appearance that in the small town of Progrody he was known not by his name, which had gradually fallen into disuse, but by his calling. For instance, people would say: "Here comes the coral merchant"—as though there were none but him in all the world.

And in fact, Nissen Piczenik did feel a kind of affinity or kinship with corals. He had never been to school, couldn't read or write, and was only able to mark his name crudely; but he lived with the wholly unscientific conviction that corals were not plants at all, but living creatures, a kind of tiny reddish sea animal, and no professor of marine science could have convinced him otherwise. Yes, for Nissen Piczenik corals remained alive, even when they had been sawn, cut, polished, sorted, and threaded. And perhaps he was right. Because with his own eyes he had seen how on the breasts of sick or poorly women his reddish strings of corals would begin to fade, while on the breasts of healthy women they kept their luster. In the course of his long experience as a coral merchant, he had often observed how corals that — for all their redness — had grown pale from lying in cupboards, once they were put round the neck of a healthy and beautiful young peasant woman, would start to glow as if they drew nourishment from the woman's blood. Sometimes, the merchant was offered corals to buy back, and he recognized the stones he had once threaded and cherished — and he could tell right away whether the woman who had worn them had been healthy or unhealthy.

He had a very particular theory of his own regarding corals. As already stated, he thought of them as sea creatures, who as it were, out of prudence and modesty, only imitated plants and trees so as to avoid being attacked and eaten by sharks. It was every coral's dream to be plucked by a diver and brought to the surface, to be cut, polished, and threaded, so as finally to be able to serve the purpose for which it had been created: namely to be an ornament on a beautiful peasant woman. Only there, on the fine, firm white throat of a woman, in close proximity to the living artery — sister of the feminine heart — did they revive, acquire luster and beauty, and exercise their innate ability to charm men and awaken their ardor. Now, the ancient god Jehovah had created everything, the earth and the beasts who walked upon it, the sea and all its creatures. But for the time being — namely, until the coming of the Messiah — he had left the supervision of all the animals and plants of the sea, and in particular of corals, to the care of the Leviathan, who lay curled on the seabed.

It might be supposed that the trader Nissen Piczenik had a reputation as something of an eccentric. Nothing could be further from the truth. Piczenik lived quietly and unobtrusively in the small town of Progrody, and his tales of corals and the Leviathan were treated with complete seriousness, as befitting the opinion of an expert, a man who must know his business, just as the haberdasher knew his German percale from his corduroy, and the tea merchant could tell the Russian tea from the famous firm of Popov from the English tea supplied by the equally famous firm of Liptons of London. All the inhabitants of Progrody and its surroundings were convinced that corals are living creatures, and that the great fish Leviathan was responsible for their well-being under the sea. There could be no question of that, since Nissen Piczenik said so himself.

In Nissen Piczenik's house, the beautiful threaders often worked far into the night, sometimes even past midnight. Once they had gone home, the trader himself sat down with his stones, or rather, his animals. First, he examined the strings the girls had threaded; then he counted the heaps of corals that were as yet unsorted and the heaps of those that had been sorted according to type and size; then he began sorting them himself, and with his strong and deft and reddish-haired fingers, he felt and smoothed and stroked each individual coral. There were some corals that were worm-eaten. They had holes in places where no holes were required. The sloppy Leviathan couldn't have been paying attention. And reproachfully, Nissen Piczenik lit a candle, and held a piece of red wax over the flame until it melted, and then dipping a fine needle into the wax, he sealed the wormholes in the stone, all the while shaking his head, as though not comprehending how such a powerful god as Jehovah could have left such an irresponsible fish as the Leviathan in charge of all the corals.

Sometimes, out of pure pleasure in the stones, he would thread corals himself until the sky grew light and it was time for him to say his morning prayers. The work didn't tire him at all, he felt strong and alert. His wife was still under the blankets, asleep. He gave her a curt, indifferent look. He didn't love her or hate her, she was merely one of the many threaders who worked for him, though she was less attractive now than most of the others. Ten years he had been married to her, and she had borne him no children — when that alone was her function. He wanted a fertile woman, fertile as the sea on whose bed so many corals grew. His wife, though, was like a dried-up lake. Let her sleep alone, as many nights as she wanted. According to the law, he could divorce her. But by now he had become indifferent to wives and children. Corals were what he loved. And there was in his heart a vague longing which he couldn't quite explain: Nissen Piczenik, born and having lived all his life in the middle of a great landmass, longed for the sea.

Yes, he longed for the sea on whose bed the corals grew — or rather, as he was convinced, disported themselves. Far and wide there was no one to whom he could speak of his longing; he had to carry it pent up in himself, as the sea carries its corals. He had heard about ships and divers, sailors and sea captains. His corals arrived, still smelling of the sea, in neatly packed crates from Odessa, Hamburg, and Trieste. The public scribe in the post office did his correspondence for him. Nissen Piczenik carefully examined the colorful stamps on the letters from his suppliers abroad before throwing away the envelopes. He had never left Progrody. The town didn't have a river, not so much as a pond, only swamps on all sides, where you could hear the water gurgle far below the green surface without being able to see it. Nissen Piczenik imagined some secret communication between the buried water in the swamps and the mighty waters of the sea—and that deep down at the bottom of the swamp, there might be corals, too. He knew that if he ever said as much, he would be a laughingstock all over town. And so he kept his silence, and didn't talk about his theories. Sometimes he dreamed that the Great Sea—he didn't know which one, he had never seen a map, and so where he was concerned, all the world's seas were just the Great Sea—would one day flood Russia, the part of it where he lived himself. That way, the sea, which he had no hope of reaching, would come to him, the strange and mighty sea, with the immeasurable Leviathan on the bottom, and all its sweet and bitter and salty secrets.

The road from the small town of Progrody to the little railway station where trains called just three times a week led through the swamps. And even when Nissen Piczenik wasn't expecting any packages of coral, even on days when there weren't any trains, he would walk to the station, or rather, to the swamps. He would stand often for an hour or more at the edge of the swamp and listen reverently to the croaking of the frogs, as if they could tell him of life at the bottom of the swamp, and sometimes he felt he had taken their meaning. In winter, when the swamp froze over, he even dared to take a few steps on it, and that gave him a peculiar delight. The moldy swamp smell seemed to convey something of the powerful briny aroma of the sea, and to his eager ears the miserable glugging of the buried waters was transformed into the roaring of enormous green-blue breakers.

In the whole small town of Progrody there was no one who knew what was going on in the soul of the coral merchant. All the Jews took him for just another one like themselves. This man dealt in cloth, and that one in kerosene; one sold prayer shawls, another soaps and wax candles, and a third, kerchiefs for farmers' wives and pocket knives; one taught the children how to pray, another how to count, and a third sold kvas and beans and roasted maize kernels. And to all of them Nissen Piczenik seemed one of themselves — with the only difference that he happened to deal in coral. And yet — you will see — he was altogether different.

II

HIS CUSTOMERS WERE both rich and poor, regular and occasional. Among his rich customers were two local farmers. One of them, Timon Semyonovitch, was a hop grower, and every year when the buyers came down from Nuremberg and Zatec and Judenburg, he made a number of profitable deals. The other farmer was Nikita Ivanovitch. He had no fewer than eight daughters, whom he was marrying off one after the other, and all needed corals. The married daughters — to date there were four of them — a month or two after their weddings gave birth to children of their own — more daughters — and these too required corals, though they were only infants, to ward off the Evil Eye.

The members of these two families were the most esteemed guests in Nissen Piczenik's house. For the daughters of these farmers, their sons-in-law and their grandchildren, the merchant kept a supply of good brandy in reserve, homemade brandy flavored with ants, dried mushrooms, parsley, and centaury. The ordinary customers had to be content with ordinary shop-bought vodka. For in that part of the world there was no purchasing anything without a drink. Buyer and seller drank to the transaction, that it might bring profit and blessing to both parties. There were also heaps of loose tobacco in the apartment of the coral merchant, lying by the window, wrapped in damp blotting paper to keep it fresh. For customers didn't come to Nissen Piczenik the way people go into a shop, merely to buy the goods, pay, and leave. The majority of the customers had covered many versts, and to Nissen Piczenik they were more than customers, they were also his guests. They drank with him, smoked with him, and sometimes even ate with him. The merchant's wife prepared buckwheat kasha with onions, borscht with sour cream, she roasted apples and potatoes, and chestnuts in the autumn. And so the customers were not just customers, they were guests of Nissen Piczenik's house. Sometimes, while they were hunting for suitable corals, the farmers' wives would join in the singing of the threaders; then they all would sing together, and even Nissen Piczenik would hum to himself, and in the kitchen his wife would beat time with a wooden spoon. Then, when the farmers returned from the market or from the inn to pick up their wives and pay for their purchases, the coral merchant would be obliged to drink brandy or tea with them, and smoke a cigarette. And all the old customers would kiss the merchant on both cheeks like a brother.

Because once we have got a drink or two inside us, all good honest men are our brothers, and all fair women our sisters — and there is no difference between farmer and merchant, Jew and Christian; and woe to anyone who says otherwise!

III

WITH EVERY YEAR that passed, unbeknownst to anyone in the small town of Progrody, Nissen Piczenik grew
more dissatisfied with his uneventful life. Like every other
Jew, the coral merchant went to synagogue twice a day,
morning and evening, he celebrated holidays, fasted on
fast days, he put on his prayer shawl and his phylacter-
ies, and swayed back and forth from the waist, he talked to
people, he had conversations about politics, about the war
with Japan, about what was printed in the newspapers and
preoccupying the world. But deep in his heart, there was
still the longing for the sea, home of the corals, and not being able to read, he asked to have read out to him any items
relating to the sea when the newspapers came to Progrody
twice a week. Just as he did about corals, he had a very particular notion of the sea. He knew that strictly speaking the
world had many seas, but the one true sea was the one you
had to cross in order to reach America.

Now it happened one day that the son of the hessian
seller Alexander Komrower, who three years previously
had enlisted and joined the navy, returned home for a
short leave. No sooner had the coral merchant got to

hear of young Komrower's return than he appeared in his house and started asking the sailor about all the mysteries of ships, water, and winds. Whereas the rest of Progrody was convinced that it had been sheer stupidity that had got young Komrower hauled off to the dangerous oceans, the coral merchant saw in the sailor a fortunate youth, who had been granted the favor and the distinction of being made, as it were, an intimate of the corals, yes, even a kind of relation. And so the forty-five-year-old Nissen Piczenik and the twenty-two-year-old Komrower were seen walking about arm-in-arm in the marketplace of the little town for hours on end. People asked themselves: What does he want with that Komrower? And the young fellow asked himself: What does he want with me?

During the whole period of the young man's leave in Progrody, the coral merchant hardly left his side. Their exchanges, like the following, were bewildering to the younger man:

"Can you see down to the bottom of the sea with a telescope?"

"No," replied the sailor, "with a telescope you only look into the distance, not into the deep."

"Can you," Nissen Piczenik went on, "as a sailor, go down to the bottom of the sea?"

"No," said young Komrower, "except if you drown, then you might well go down to the bottom."

"What about the captain?"

"The captain can't either."

"Have you ever seen a diver?"

"A few times," said the sailor.

"Do sea creatures and sea plants sometimes climb up to the surface?"

"Only some fish like whales that aren't really fish at all."

"Describe the sea to me!" said Nissen Piczenik.

"It's full of water," said the sailor Komrower.

"And is it very wide and flat, like a great steppe with no houses on it?"

"It's as wide as that—and more!" said the young sailor. "And it's just like you say: a wide plain, with the odd house dotted about on it, only not a house but a ship."

"Where did you see divers?"

"We in the navy," said the young man, "have got our own divers. But they don't dive for pearls or oysters or corals. It's for military purposes, for instance, in case a warship goes down, and then they can retrieve important instruments or weapons."

"How many seas are there?"

"I wouldn't know, " replied the sailor. "We were told at navy school, but I didn't pay any attention. The only ones I know are the Baltic, the Black Sea, and the Great Ocean."

"Which sea is the deepest?"

"Don't know."

"Where are the most corals found?"

"Don't know that, either."

"Hmm, hmm," said the coral merchant. "Pity you don't know that."

At the edge of the small town, there where the little houses of Progrody grew ever more wretched until they

17

finally petered out altogether, and the wide humpbacked road to the station began, stood Podgorzev's bar, a house of ill-repute in which peasants, farm laborers, soldiers, stray girls, and layabouts congregated. One day, the coral merchant Piczenik was seen going in there with the sailor Komrower. They were served strong, dark red mead and salted peas. "Drink, my boy! Eat and drink, my boy!" said Nissen Piczenik to the sailor in fatherly fashion. And the boy ate and drank for all he was worth, for young as he was, he had already learned a thing or two in ports, and after the mead he was given some bad sour wine, and after the wine a 90-proof brandy. He was so quiet over the mead that the coral merchant feared he had heard all he was going to hear on the subject of the sea from the sailor, and that his knowledge was simply exhausted. After the wine, however, young Komrower got into conversation with the barkeeper, and when the 90-proof brandy came, he fell to singing at the top of his voice, one song after another, just like a real sailor.

"Do you hail from our beloved little town?" asked the barkeeper. "Of course, I'm a child of your — my — our little town," replied the sailor, as if he wasn't the son of the plump Jew Komrower, but a regular farmer's boy. A couple of tramps and ne'er-do-wells came over to join Nissen Piczenik and the sailor at their table, and when the boy saw he had an audience, he felt a keen sense of dignity, such dignity as he thought only ships' officers could possibly have. And he played up to them: "Go on, fellows, ask all you like. I've got answers to all your questions. You see this dear old uncle here, you all know who he is, he's the best coral seller in the whole province, and I've told him a lot of things already!" Nissen Piczenik nodded. And since he felt uneasy in this unfamiliar company, he drank a glass of mead, and then another. Gradually, all these dubious faces he'd previously only seen through the grille in his door became as human as his own. But as caution and suspicion were ingrained in his nature, he went out into the yard and hid his purse in his cap, leaving only a few coins loose in his pocket. Satisfied with his idea, and soothed by the pressure of the money against his skull, he sat down at the table again.

And yet he had to admit to himself that he didn't really know what he was doing, sitting in the bar with the sailor and these criminal types. All his life he had kept himself to himself, and prior to the arrival of the sailor, his secret passion for corals and the ocean home of corals had not been made public in any way. And there was something else that alarmed Nissen Piczenik deeply. He suddenly saw his secret longing for waters and whatever lived in them and upon them as coming to the surface of his own life, like some rare and precious creature at home on the seabed shooting up to the surface for some unknown reason — and he had never had such vivid thoughts before. The sudden fancy must have been prompted by the mead and the stimulating effect of the sailor's stories. The fact that such crazy notions could come to him upset and alarmed him even more than suddenly finding himself sitting at a bar-room table among vice-ridden associates.

Joseph Roth

But all his alarm and upset remained submerged, well below the surface of his mind. All the while, he was listening with keen enjoyment to the incredible tales of the sailor Komrower. "And what about your own ship?" his new friends were asking him. The sailor thought about it for awhile. His ship was named after a famous nineteenth-century admiral, but that name seemed as banal as his own, and Komrower was determined to impress them all mightily—and so he said: "My cruiser is called the *Little Mother Catherine*. Do you know who she was? Of course you don't, so I'll tell you. Well, then, Catherine was the richest and most beautiful woman in the whole of Russia, and so one day the Tsar married her in the Kremlin in Moscow, and then he took her away on a sleigh—it was forty below—drawn by six horses to Tsarskoye Selo. Behind them came their whole retinue on sleighs—and there were so many of them, the road was blocked for three days and three nights. Then, a week after the magnificent wedding, the wanton and aggressive King of Sweden arrived in Petersburg harbor with his ridiculous wooden barges, but with a lot of soldiers standing up on them because the Swedes are very brave fighters on land—and this king had a plan to conquer the whole of Russia. So the Tsarina Catherine straightway got on a ship, namely, the very cruiser I'm serving on, and with her own hands she bombed the silly barges of the King of Sweden and sank the lot of them. And she tossed the King a life belt and took him prisoner. She had his eyes put out and ate them, and that made her even more clever than she was before.

As for the blind King, he was packed off to Siberia."

"Is that so?" said one of the layabouts, scratching his head. "I can't hardly believe it."

"You say that again," retorted the sailor Komrower, "and I'll be obliged to kill you for insulting the Imperial Russian Navy. I'll have you know I learned this whole story at our Naval Academy, and His Grace, our Captain Voroshenko, told it to us in person."

They drank some more mead and one or two more brandies, and then the coral merchant Nissen Piczenik paid for everyone. He had had a few drinks himself, though not as many as the others. But when he stepped out onto the street, arm-in-arm with the young sailor Komrower, it seemed to him as though the middle of the road was a river with waves rippling up and down it, the occasional oil lanterns were lighthouses, and he had better stick to the side of the road if he wasn't to fall into the water. The young fellow was swaying all over the place. Now, from his childhood days, Nissen Piczenik had said his prayers every evening, the one that you say when it starts to get dark, the other one at nightfall. Today, for the first time, he had missed them both. The stars were twinkling reproachfully at him up in the sky, he didn't dare look at them. At home his wife would be waiting with his usual evening meal, radish with cucumbers and onions, a piece of bread and dripping, a glass of kvas and hot tea. He felt more shame on his own behalf than in front of other people. He had the feeling, walking along arm-in-arm with the heavy, stumbling young man, that he was con-

Joseph Roth

tinually running into himself, the coral merchant Nissen Piczenik was meeting the coral merchant Nissen Piczenik, and they were laughing at one another. However, he was able to avoid meeting anyone else. He brought young Komrower home, took him into the room where the old Komrowers were sitting, and said: "Don't be angry with him. I went to the bar with him, he's had a bit to drink."

"You, Nissen Piczenik, the coral merchant, have been drinking with him?" asked old Komrower.

"Yes, I have!" said Piczenik. "Now, good night!" And he went home. His beautiful threaders were still all sitting at the four long tables singing and fishing up corals with their delicate needles in their fine hands.

"Just give me some tea," said Nissen Piczenik to his wife. "I have work to do."

And he drank his tea, and while his hot fingers scrabbled about in the large, still unsorted heaps of corals, and in their delicious rosy cool, his poor heart was wandering over the wide and roaring highways of the mighty ocean.

And there was a mighty burning and roaring in his skull. Sensibly, though, he remembered to take off his cap, pull out his purse, and put it back in his shirt once more.

IV

THE DAY DREW nigh when the sailor Komrower was to report back to his cruiser in Odessa — and the coral merchant dreaded the prospect. In all Progrody, young Komrower is the only sailor, and God knows when he'll be given leave again. Once he goes, that'll be the last you hear of the waters of the world, apart from the odd item in the newspapers.

The summer was well advanced, a fine summer, by the way, cloudless and dry, cooled by the steady breeze across the Volhynian steppes. Another two weeks and it would be harvest time, and the peasants would no longer be coming in from their villages on market days to buy corals from Nissen Piczenik. These two weeks were the height of the coral season. In this fortnight the customers came in great bunches and clusters, the threaders could hardly keep up with the work, they stayed up all night sorting and threading. In the beautiful early evenings, when the declining sun sent its golden adieus through Piczenik's barred windows, and the heaps of coral of every type and hue, animated by its melancholy and bracing light, started to glow as though each little stone carried its own microscopic lantern in its delicate interior, the farmers would turn up boisterous and a little merry, to collect their wives, with their red and blue handkerchiefs filled with silver and copper coins, in heavy hobnailed boots that clattered on the cobbles in the yard outside. The farmers greeted Nissen Piczenik with embraces and kisses, like a long-lost friend. They meant well by him, they were even fond of him, the lanky, taciturn, red-haired Jew with the honest, sometimes wistful china blue eyes, where decency lived and fair dealing, the savvy of the expert and the ignorance of the man who had never once left the small town of Progrody. It wasn't easy to get the better of the farmers. For although they recognized the coral merchant as one of the few honest tradesmen in the area, they wouldn't forget that he was a Jew. And they weren't averse to haggling themselves. First, they made themselves at home on the chairs, the settee, the two wide wooden double beds with plump bolsters on them. And some of them, their boots encrusted with silvery-gray mud, even lay down on the beds, the sofa, or the floor. They took pinches of loose tobacco from the pockets of their burlap trousers, or from the supplies on the windowsill, tore off the edges of old newspapers that were lying around in Piczenik's room, and rolled themselves cigarettes — cigarette papers were considered a luxury, even by the well-off among them. Soon, the coral merchant's apartment was filled with the dense blue smoke of cheap tobacco and rough paper, blue smoke gilded by the last of the sunlight, gradually emptying itself out into the street in small clouds drifting through the squares of the barred open windows.

24

In a couple of copper samovars on a table in the middle of the room—these too burnished by the setting sun—hot water was kept boiling, and no fewer than fifty cheap green double-bottomed glasses were passed from hand to hand, full of schnapps and steaming golden-brown tea. The prices of the coral necklaces had already been agreed on with the women in the course of several hours' bargaining in the morning. But now the husbands were unhappy with the price, and so the haggling began all over again. It was a hard struggle for the skinny Jew, all on his own against overwhelming numbers of tightfisted and suspicious, strongly built and in their cups potentially violent men. The sweat ran down under the black silk cap he wore at home, down his freckled, thinly bearded cheeks into the red goatee, and the hairs of his beard grew matted together, so that in the evening, after the battle, he had to part them with a little fine-toothed steel comb. Finally, he won the day against his customers, in spite of his ignorance. For, in the whole wide world, there were only two things that he understood, which were corals and the farmers of the region—and he knew how to thread the former and outwit the latter. The implacably obstinate ones would be given a so-called extra—in other words, when they agreed to pay the price he had secretly been hoping for all along, he would give them a tiny coral chain made from stones of little value, to put round the necks or wrists of their children, where it was guaranteed to be effective against the Evil Eye or spiteful neighbors and wicked witches. And all the time he had to watch what the hands of his customers were up to, and to keep gauging the size of the various piles of coral. It really wasn't easy!

In this particular high summer, however, Nissen Picze-nik's manner was distracted, almost apathetic. He seemed indifferent to his customers and to his business. His loyal wife, long accustomed to his peculiar silences, noticed the change in him and took him to task. He had sold a string of corals too cheaply here, he had failed to spot a little theft there, today he had given an old customer no "extras," while yesterday he'd given a new and insignificant buyer quite a valuable necklace. There had never been any strife in the Piczenik household. But over the course of these days, the coral merchant lost his calm, and he felt himself how his indifference, his habitual indifference toward his wife suddenly turned into violent dislike. Yes, he who was incapable of drowning a single one of the many mice that were caught in his traps every night — the way everyone in Progrody did — but instead paid Saul the water carrier to do it for him, on this day, he, the peaceable Nissen Piczenik, threw a heavy string of corals in his wife's face as she was criticizing him as usual, slammed the door, and walked out of the house to sit by the edge of the great swamp, the cousin many times removed of the great oceans.

Just two days before the sailor's departure, there sur-faced in the coral merchant the notion of accompanying young Komrower to Odessa. A notion like that arrives suddenly, lightning is slow by comparison, and it hits the very place from where it sprang, which is to say the hu-man heart. If you like, it strikes its own birthplace. Such was Nissen Piczenik's notion. And from such a notion to a resolution is only a short distance.

On the morning of the departure of the young sailor Komrower, Nissen Piczenik said to his wife: "I have to go away for a few days."

His wife was still in bed. It was eight in the morning, the coral merchant had just returned from morning prayers in the synagogue.

She sat up. Without her wig on, her thin hair in disarray and yellow crusts of sleep in the corners of her eyes, she looked unfamiliar, even hostile to him. Her appearance, her alarm, her consternation all confirmed him in a decision which even to him had seemed rash.

"I'm going to Odessa!" he said with unconcealed venom. "I'll be back in a week, God willing!"

"Now? Now?" stammered his wife amongst the pillows. "Does it have to be now, when all the farmers are coming?"

"Right now!" said the coral merchant. "I have important business. Pack my things!"

And with a vicious and spiteful delight he had never previously felt, he watched as his wife got out of bed, saw her ugly toes, her fat legs below the long flea-spotted nightgown, and he heard her all-too familiar sigh, the inevitable morning song of this woman with whom nothing connected him beyond the distant memory of a few nocturnal tendernesses, and the usual fear of divorce.

But within Nissen Piczenik there was a jubilant voice, a strange and familiar voice inside him: Piczenik is off to the corals! He's off to the corals! Nissen Piczenik is going to the home of the corals! ...

V

SO HE BOARDED the train with the sailor Komrower and went to Odessa. It was a long and complicated journey, with a change at Kiev. It was the first time the coral merchant had been on a train, but he didn't feel about it the way most people do when they ride on a train for the first time. The locomotive, the signals, the bells, the telegraph masts, the tracks, the conductors, and the landscape flying by outside, none of it interested him. He was preoccupied with water and the harbor he was headed for, and if he registered any of the characteristic features of railway travel, it was only in order to speculate on the still unfamiliar features of travel on board ship. "Do you have bells, too?" he asked the sailor. "Do they ring three times before the ship leaves? Does the ship have to turn round, or can it just swim backward?"

Of course, as inevitably happens on journeys, they met other passengers who wanted to get into conversation, and so he had to discuss this and that with them. "I'm a coral merchant," said Nissen Piczenik truthfully, when he was asked what it was he did. But when the next question came: "What brings you to Odessa?" he began to lie.

"I have some important business there." "How interesting," said a fellow passenger, who until that moment had said nothing, "I, too, have important business in Odessa, and the merchandise I deal in is not unrelated to coral, although it is of course far finer and dearer." "Dearer it may be," said Nissen Piczenik, "but it can't possibly be finer!" "You want to bet it isn't?" cried the man. "I tell you it's impossible. There's no point in betting!" Well then," crowed the man, "I deal in pearls." "Pearls aren't at all finer," said Piczenik. "And besides, they're unlucky." "They are if you lose them," said the pearl trader.

By now, everyone was listening to this extraordinary dispute. Finally, the pearl merchant reached into his trousers and took out a bag full of gleaming, flawless pearls. He tipped a few into the palm of his hand, and showed them to the other travelers. "To find a single pearl," he said, "hundreds of oyster shells have to be opened. The divers command very high wages. Among all the merchants of the world, we pearl traders are the most highly regarded. You could say we're a special breed. Take me, for example. I'm a merchant of the first guild, I live in Petersburg, I have a distinguished clientèle, including two Grand Dukes whose names are a trade secret, I've traveled halfway round the world, every year I go to Paris, Brussels, and Amsterdam. Ask anywhere for the pearl trader Gorodotzky, even little children will be able to direct you."

"And I," said Nissen Piczenik, "have never left our small town of Progrody, and all my customers are farmers. But you will agree that a simple farmer's wife, decked out in a couple of chains of fine, flawless corals, is not outdone by a Grand Duchess. Corals are worn by high and low alike, they raise the low and grace the high. You can wear corals morning, noon, and night, wear them to ceremonial balls, in summer and in winter, on the Sabbath and on weekdays, to work and in the home, in times happy and sad. There are many different varieties of red, my dear fellow passengers, and it is written that our Jewish king Solomon had a very special kind for his royal robes, because the Phoenicians who revered him had made him a present of a special kind of worm that excretes red dye in its urine. You can't get this color anymore, the purple of the Tsars is not the same, because after Solomon's death the whole species of that worm became extinct. Nowadays, it is only in the very reddest corals that the color still exists. Now who ever heard of such a thing as red pearls?"

Never had the quiet coral merchant held such a long and impassioned address in front of a lot of complete strangers. He put his cap back and mopped his brow. He smiled round at his fellow passengers, and they all applauded him: "He's right, he's right!" they all exclaimed at once.

And even the pearl merchant had to admit that, whatever the facts of the case, Nissen Piczenik had been an excellent advocate of corals.

They finally reached the glittering port city of Odessa, with its blue water and its host of bridal-white ships. Here the armored cruiser was waiting for the sailor Komrower, as a father's house awaits his son. Nissen Piczenik wanted very much to have a closer look at the ship. He went with the young fellow to the man on watch and said, "I'm his uncle, can I see the ship?" His own temerity surprised him. Oh yes, this wasn't the old terrestrial Nissen Piczenik who was addressing an armed sailor, it wasn't Nissen Piczenik from landlocked Progrody, this was somebody else, a man transformed, a man whose insides were now proudly on the outside, an oceanic Nissen Piczenik. It seemed to him that he hadn't just got off the train, but that he had climbed out of the water, out of the depths of the Black Sea. He felt at home by the water, as he had never felt at home in Progrody, where he was born and had lived all his life. Wherever he looks, he sees nothing but ships and water, water and ships. There are the ships, the boats, the tugs, the yachts, the motorboats apple blossom white, raven black, coral red, yes, coral red — and there is the water washing against their sides, no, not washing but lapping and stroking, in thousands of little wavelets, like tongues and hands at once. The Black Sea isn't black at all. In the distance, it's bluer than the sky; close to, it's as green as grass. When you toss a piece of bread in the water, thousands and thousands of swift little fishes leap, skip, slip, slither, flit, and flash to the spot. A cloudless blue sky arches over the harbor, pricked by the masts and chimneys of the ships. "What's this? What's the name of that?" asks Nissen Piczenik incessantly. This is a mast, that's a bow, these are the life preservers, there is a difference between a boat and a barge, a sailing vessel and a steamship, a mast and a funnel, a battleship and a merchantman, deck and stern, bow and keel. Nissen Piczenik's poor undaunted brain is bombarded by hundreds of new terms. After a long wait—he is very lucky, says the first mate—he is given permission to accompany his nephew on board, and to inspect the cruiser. This ship's lieutenant appears in person to watch a Jewish merchant go on board a vessel of the Imperial Russian Fleet. His Honor the lieutenant is pleased to smile. The long black skirts of the lanky red-haired Jew flutter in the gentle breeze, his striped trousers show, worn and patched, tucked into scuffed boots. The Jew Nissen Piczenik even forgets the laws of his faith. He doffs his black cap in front of the brilliant white and gold glory of the officer, and his red curls fly in the wind. "Your nephew's a fine lad," says His Honor, the officer, and Nissen Piczenik can think of no suitable reply. He smiles, he doesn't laugh, he smiles silently. His mouth is open, revealing his big yellow horsey teeth and his pink gums, and the copper-colored goatee drops down almost to his chest. He inspects the wheel, the cannons, he's allowed to peer down the ship's telescope—and by God, the far is brought near, what is a long way off is made to seem close at hand, in that glass. God gave man eyes, but what are ordinary eyes compared to eyes looking through a telescope? God gave man eyes, but He also gave him understanding that he might invent the telescope and improve the power of his eyesight! And the sun shines down on the top deck, it shines on Nissen Piczenik's back, and still he doesn't grow hot, for there is a cooling breeze blowing over the sea, yes, it's as though the wind came out of the sea itself, a wind out of the very depths of the sea.

Finally, the hour of parting came. Nissen Piczenik embraced young Komrower, he bowed to the lieutenant and then to the sailors, and he left the battle cruiser.

He had intended to return to Progrody straight after saying good-bye to young Komrower. But he remained in Odessa. He watched the battleship sail off, the sailors waved back to him as he stood on the quay side, waving his red and blue–striped handkerchief. And he watched a lot of other ships sailing away, and he waved to their passengers as well. He went to the harbor every day, and every day he saw something new. For instance, he learned what it means to "lift anchor," "furl the sails," "unload a cargo," "tighten a sheet," and so forth.

Every day he saw young men in sailor suits working on ships, swarming up the masts, he saw young men walking through the streets of Odessa, arm-in-arm, a line of sailors walking abreast, taking up the whole street—and he felt sad that he had no children of his own. Just then, he wished he had sons and grandsons and—no question— he would have sent them all to sea. He'd have made sailors of them. And all the while his ugly and infertile wife was lying at home in Progrody. She was selling corals in his place. Did she know how? Did she have any appreciation of what corals meant?

In the port of Odessa, Nissen Piczenik rapidly forgot the obligations of an ordinary Jew from Progrody. He didn't go to the synagogue in the morning to say the prescribed prayers, nor yet in the evening. Instead, he prayed at home, hurriedly, without proper thought of God, he

prayed in the manner of a phonograph, his tongue mechanically repeating the sounds that were engraved in his
brain. Had the world ever seen such a Jew?

At home in Progrody, it was the coral season. Nissen
Piczenik knew it, but then he wasn't the old continental
Nissen Piczenik any more, he was the new, reborn, oce-
anic one.

There's plenty of time to go back to Progrody, he told
himself. I'm not missing anything. Think of what I still
have to do here!

And he stayed in Odessa for three weeks, and every day
he spent happy hours with the sea and the ships and the
little fishes.

It was the first time in his life that Nissen Piczenik had
had a holiday.

VI

WHEN HE RETURNED home to Progrody, he discovered that he was no less than one hundred and sixty rubles out of pocket, with all the expenses for his journey. But to his wife and to all those who asked him what he had been doing so long away from home, he replied that he had concluded some "important business" in Odessa.

The harvest was just now getting underway, and so the farmers didn't come to town so frequently on market days. As happened every year at this time, it grew quiet in the house of the coral merchant. The threaders went home in the afternoon. And in the evening, when Nissen Piczenik returned from the synagogue, he was greeted not by the melodious voices of the beautiful girls, but only by his wife, his plate of radish and onion, and the copper samovar. However, guided by the memory of his days in Odessa—whose commercial insignificance he kept secret—the coral merchant Piczenik bowed to the habitual rules of his autumnal days. Already he was thinking of claiming some further piece of important business in a few months' time, and going to visit a different harbor town, Petersburg, for instance.

He had no financial problems. All the money he had earned in the course of many years of selling corals was deposited and earning steady interest with the money-lender Pinkas Warschawsky, a respected usurer in the community, who, though pitiless in collecting any out-standing debts owing to him, was also punctual in paying interest. Nissen Piczenik had no material anxieties; he was childless and had no heirs to think of, so why not travel to another of the many harbors there were?

And the coral dealer had already begun to make plans for the spring when something strange happened in the small neighboring town of Sutschky.

In this town, which was no bigger than the small town of Progrody, the home of Nissen Piczenik, a complete stranger one day opened a coral shop. The man's name was Jenö Lakatos, and, as was soon learned, he came from the distant land of Hungary. He spoke Russian, German, Ukrainian, and Polish, and yes, if required, and if some-one had happened to ask for it, then Mr. Lakatos would equally have spoken in French, English, or Chinese. He was a young man with slick, blue-black, pomaded hair — and he was also the only man far and wide to wear a shiny stiff collar and tie, and to carry a walking stick with a gold knob. This young man had been in Sutschky for just a few weeks, had struck up a friendship with the butcher Nikita Kolchin, and had pestered him for so long that he agreed to set up a coral business jointly with this Lakatos. There was a brilliant red sign outside with the name NIKITA KOLCHIN & CO.

In its window, this shop displayed perfect shining red corals, lighter in weight than the stones of Nissen Piczenik, but also cheaper. A whole large coral necklace cost one ruble fifty, and there were smaller chains for eighty, fifty and twenty kopecks. The prices were prominently displayed in the window. Finally, to prevent anyone still walking past the shop, there was a phonograph inside turning out merry tunes all day long. It could be heard all over town, and in the outlying villages, too. There was no large market in Sutschky as there was in Progrody. Nevertheless — and in spite of the fact that it was harvest time — the farmers flocked to the shop of Mr. Lakatos to hear the music and buy the cheap corals.

One day, after Mr. Lakatos had been running his business successfully for a few weeks, a prosperous farmer came to Nissen Piczenik and said: "Nissen Semyonovitch, I can't believe the way you've been cheating me and everybody else these past twenty years. But now there's a man in Sutschky who's selling the most beautiful coral chains for fifty kopecks apiece. My wife wanted to go over there right away, but I thought I'd see what you had to say about it first, Nissen Semyonovitch."

"That Lakatos," said Nissen Piczenik, "is a thief and a cheat. There's no other way to explain his prices. But I'll go over there if you give me a lift in your cart."

"Very well," said the farmer, "see for yourself."

And so the coral merchant went to Sutschky. He stood in front of the shop window for awhile, listening to the music blaring from inside the shop, then finally he stepped inside, and addressed Mr. Lakatos.

"I'm a coral seller myself," said Nissen Piczenik. "My wares come from Hamburg, Odessa, Trieste, and Amsterdam, and I can't understand how you are able to sell such fine corals so cheaply."

"You're from the old school," replied Lakatos, "and if you'll pardon the expression, you're a bit behind the times."

So saying, he emerged from behind the counter—and Nissen Piczenik saw that he had a slight limp. His left leg was obviously shorter, because the heel of his left boot was twice as high as the one on his right. Powerful and intoxicating scents emanated from him—and one wondered what part of his frail body could possibly be home to all these scents. His hair was blackish-blue as night. And while his dark eyes appeared gentle enough, they glowed so powerfully that a strange redness appeared to flare up in the midst of all their blackness. Under his curled black mustaches, Lakatos had a set of dazzling white and smiling mouse teeth.

"Well?" said the coral merchant Nissen Piczenik.

"Well," said Lakatos, "we're not mad. We don't go diving to the bottom of the sea. We simply manufacture artificial corals. I work for the company of Lowncastle Brothers, in New York. I've just had two very good years in Budapest. It doesn't bother the farmers. It didn't bother them in Hungary, it'll never bother them in Russia. Fine red flawless corals are what they're after. And I've got them. Cheap, competitively priced, pretty, and wearable. What more do they want? Real corals don't come any better!"

"What are your corals made of?" asked Nissen Piczenik.

"Celluloid, my dear fellow, celluloid!" cried a delighted Lakatos. "It's no good arguing with science! Anyway, rubber trees grow in Africa, and it's rubber that you make celluloid out of. What's unnatural about that? Are rubber trees any less part of nature than corals? How is a rubber tree in Africa any worse than a coral tree on the seabed? Well, so what do you say? Do you want to do a deal with me? Just say the word! A year from now, all your customers will have gone over to me, and you can take all your fine real corals back to the seabed they came from. So, will you come in with me or not?"

"Give me two days to think it over," said Nissen Piczenik, and he went home.

VII

AND THAT WAS how the Devil first came to tempt the coral merchant Nissen Piczenik. The Devil was Jenö Lakatos from Budapest, who introduced artificial coral to Russia — celluloid coral that burns with a bluish flame, the same color as the ring of purgatorial fire that burns around Hell.

When Nissen Piczenik got home, he kissed his wife indifferently on both cheeks, he greeted his threaders, and he started looking at his beloved corals with confused eyes, eyes confused by the Devil, his living corals that didn't look nearly as flawless as the fake celluloid corals that his rival Jenö Lakatos had shown him. And so the Devil inspired the honest coral merchant Nissen Piczenik with the idea of mixing fake corals with real.

One day he went to the public clerk in the post office and dictated a letter to Jenö Lakatos in Sutschky, and a few days later he received no less than twenty *pud* of fake coral. Dazzled and led astray by the Devil, Nissen Piczenik mixed the fake and the real corals, and thereby he betrayed both himself and the real corals.

The harvest was in progress out in the countryside, and

hardly any farmers were coming to buy corals. But from the few who did occasionally turn up, Nissen Piczenik now earned more than he had before when he had had many customers, thanks to the fake corals. He mixed genuine and fake—which was even worse than selling only fake. Because that is what happens to people when they are led astray by the Devil—they come to outdo him in devilishness. And so Nissen Piczenik outdid Jenö Lakatos from Budapest. And all that Nissen Piczenik earned he took conscientiously to Pinkas Warschawsky. And so corrupted had the coral merchant been by the Devil that he took real pleasure in the thought of his money being fruitful and multiplying.

Then one day the usurer Pinkas Warschawsky suddenly died, and at that Nissen Piczenik panicked, and he went right away to the usurer's heirs, and he demanded his money back with interest. It was paid out on the spot, and the sum came to no less than five thousand four hundred and fifty rubles and sixty kopecks. With that money he paid Lakatos for his fake corals, and he ordered another twenty *pud*.

One day, the rich hop farmer came to Nissen Piczenik and asked for a chain of corals for one of his grandchildren, to ward off the Evil Eye.

The coral merchant threaded a chain made up entirely of fake corals, and he said: "These are the most beautiful corals I have."

The farmer paid him the price for real corals, and returned to the village.

A week after the fake corals had been placed round her neck, his granddaughter came down with diphtheria, and died horribly of suffocation. And in the village of Solovetzk where the rich farmer lived (and also in the surrounding villages), the news spread that the corals of Nissen Piczenik from Progrody brought bad luck and illness — and not only to those who had bought from him. For diphtheria began to rage in the surrounding villages, it took away many children, and the rumor spread that Nissen Piczenik's corals brought sickness and death.

And so that winter no more customers came to Nissen Piczenik. It was a hard winter. Every day brought with it an iron frost, hardly any snow fell, and even the rooks seemed to freeze as they crouched on the bare boughs of the chestnut trees. It grew very still in Nissen Piczenik's house. He dismissed his threaders one by one. On market days he sometimes ran into one of his old customers, but they never greeted him.

Yes, the farmers who in the summer had embraced him, now behaved as if they no longer knew the coral merchant.

The temperature fell to forty degrees below. The water froze in the water carrier's cans. A thick sheet of ice covered Nissen Piczenik's windows, so that he could no longer see what was going on in the street. Great heavy icicles hung from the crossbars of the iron grilles, and blinded the windows still further. Nissen Piczenik had no customers, but he blamed the severe winter for it, rather than the fake corals. And yet Mr. Lakatos's shop in Sutschky was continually bursting at the seams. The farmers bought his

perfect cheap celluloid corals in preference to Nissen Piczenik's real ones.

The streets of the small town of Progrody were icy and
treacherous. All the inhabitants teetered along with iron-
tipped canes. Even so, some of them fell and broke their
legs or their necks.

One evening, Nissen Piczenik's wife took a fall. She lay
there unconscious for a long time before kind neighbors
had pity on her and took her home.

She began to vomit violently. The army doctor of Progrody said she had a concussion.

She was taken to the hospital, and the doctor there confirmed the diagnosis of his army colleague.

The coral merchant visited his wife every day in the
hospital. He sat down at her bedside, listened for half an
hour to her meaningless babble, looked at her fevered
eyes, her thinning hair, remembered the few tender times
he had given her, sniffed the acrid camphor and iodine,
and went back home, stood in front of the stove and prepared borscht and kasha for himself, cut bread and grated
radish and brewed tea and lit the fire, all for himself. Then
he tipped all the corals from his many bags onto one of his
four tables, and started to sort them. Mr. Lakatos's celluloid corals he stored separately in the chest. The genuine
corals had long since ceased to be like living creatures to
Nissen Piczenik. Ever since Lakatos had turned up in the
area, and since he, the coral merchant Nissen Piczenik,
had begun mixing up the flimsy celluloid stuff with the
heavy real stones, the corals in his house were dead. Corals nowadays were made from celluloid! A dead substance

to make corals that looked like live ones, and even more beautiful and perfect than the real live ones! Compared to that, what was the concussion of his wife?

Eight days later, she died; it must have been of the effects of the concussion. But Nissen Piczenik told himself that she had not died only from her concussion, but also because her life had not been linked to that of any other human being in this world. No one had wanted her to remain alive, and so she had died.

Now the coral merchant Nissen Piczenik was a widower. He mourned his wife in the customary fashion. He bought her a relatively durable gravestone and had some pious phrases chiseled into it. He spoke the kaddish for her morning and night. But he did not miss her at all. He could make his own meals and his own tea. With his corals, he didn't feel lonely. All that saddened him was the fact that he had betrayed them to their false sisters, the celluloid corals, and himself to the dealer Lakatos.

He longed for spring, but when it came, Nissen Piczenik realized that his longing had been pointless. In former years before Easter, when the icicles started melting a little at noon, the customers had come in their creaking wagons or on their jingling sleighs. They needed corals for Easter. But now spring had come, the sun was growing warm, with every day the icicles on the roofs grew shorter and the melting piles of snow by the side of the road grew smaller — and no customers came to Nissen Piczenik. In his oaken coffer, in his wheeled trunk which stood iron-hooped and massive next to the stove, the finest corals lay in piles, bunches, and chains. But no customers came.

Joseph Roth

It grew ever warmer, the snow vanished, balmy rains fell. Violets sprang up in the woods, and frogs croaked in the swamps: no customers came.

At about this time, a certain striking transformation in the person of Nissen Piczenik was first observed in Progrody. Yes, for the first time, the people of the town began to suspect that the coral seller was an eccentric, even a peculiar fellow — and some lost their former respect for him and others laughed openly at him. Many of the good people of Progrody no longer said: "There goes the coral merchant"; instead, they said: "There goes Nissen Piczenik, he used to be a great coral merchant."

He had only himself to blame. He failed to behave in the way that the law and the dignity of widowerhood prescribed. If his strange friendship with the sailor Komrower was forgiven him, and their visit to Podgorzev's notorious bar, then his own further visits to that establishment could not be taken so lightly. For almost every day since the death of his wife, Nissen Piczenik visited Podgorzev's bar. He acquired a taste for mead, and when in time it got to be too sweet for him, he started mixing it with vodka. Sometimes, one of the girls would sit beside him. And he, who all his life had known no other woman than his now dead wife, who had taken no pleasure in anything but stroking, sorting, and threading his true loves, the corals, suddenly in Podgorzev's dive he succumbed to the cheap white flesh of women, to the pulsing of his own blood which mocked the dignity of a respectable existence, and to the wonderful narcotizing heat that radiated from the girls' bodies.

So he drank and he stroked the girls who sat next to him or occasionally even on his lap. He felt pleasure, the same pleasure he felt when playing with his corals. And with his tough, red-haired fingers he groped, less expertly — with laughable clumsiness, in fact — for the nipples of the girls, which were as rosy red as some corals. And, as they say, he let himself go more and more, practically by the day. He felt it himself. His face grew thin, his bony back grew crooked, and he no longer brushed his coat or his boots, or combed his beard. He recited his prayers mechanically every morning and evening. He felt it himself. He was no longer the coral merchant; he was Nissen Piczenik, formerly a great coral merchant.

He sensed that within a year, or maybe only six months, he would be the laughingstock of the town — but what did he care? Progrody wasn't his home, his home was the ocean.

And so one day he made the fateful decision of his life.

But before that he went back to Sutschky one day — and there in the shop of Jenö Lakatos from Budapest he saw all his old customers, and they were listening to the blaring music on the phonograph, and buying celluloid corals at fifty kopecks a chain.

"So, what did I tell you last year?" Lakatos called out to Nissen Piczenik. "You want another ten *pud*, twenty, thirty?"

Nissen Piczenik said, "I don't want any more fake corals. I only want to deal in real ones."

VIII

AND HE WENT home, back to Progrody, and he discreetly looked up the travel agent Benjamin Broczyner, who sold boat tickets to people who wanted to emigrate. These were for the most part deserters from the army or else the very poorest Jews, who had to go to Canada and America, and who provided Broczyner with his livelihood. He represented a Hamburg shipping company in Progrody.

"I want to go to Canada!" said the coral seller Nissen Piczenik. "And as soon as possible."

"The next sailing is on the *Phoenix*, which leaves Hamburg in two weeks. We can have your papers all ready by then," said Broczyner.

"Good. Good," replied Piczenik. "And I don't want anyone to know about it."

And he went home and packed all his corals, his real ones, in his wheeled suitcase.

As for the celluloid corals, he placed them on the copper tray of the samovar, and he set fire to them and watched them burning with a blue flame and a terrible stench. It took a long time: there were more than fifteen *pud* of fake corals. Indeed, all that was left of the celluloid was a gigantic heap of gray-black scrolled ashes, and a cloud of blue-gray smoke twisting round the oil lamp in the middle of the room.

That was Nissen Piczenik's farewell to his home.

On 21 April, he boarded the steamship *Phoenix* in Hamburg, as a steerage passenger.

The ship had been four days at sea when disaster struck: perhaps some still remember it.

More than two hundred passengers went down with the *Phoenix*. They were drowned, of course.

But as far as Nissen Piczenik was concerned, who went down at the same time, one cannot simply say that he was drowned along with the others. It is truer to say that he went home to the corals, to the bottom of the ocean where the huge Leviathan lies coiled.

And if we're to believe the report of a man who escaped death — as they say — by a miracle, then it appears that long before the lifeboat was filled, Nissen Piczenik leaped overboard to join his corals, his real corals.

I, for my part, willingly believe it, because I knew Nissen Piczenik, and I am ready to swear that he belonged to the corals, and that his only true home was the bottom of the ocean.

May he rest in peace beside the Leviathan until the coming of the Messiah.

Translator's Afterword

THE RADETZKY MARCH was published in September, 1932. The Jewish-Austrian novelist Joseph Roth (1894–1939) had completed his masterpiece sometime in May or June; serialization in the *Frankfurter Zeitung* had been underway since April. By Roth's standards, such a pace was sedate. *The Radetzky March* promised to transform Roth's standing, from a successful and admired newspaper writer with a sideline in (mostly bracingly short) novels, to an important contemporary novelist who once upon a time used to write for the papers. Such pleasant things as sales and advances earned-out and foreign translations for the first time loomed into prospect. It seems that Roth meant to follow his success with another major novel (which he called *meinen Erdbeeren-Roman*, "my Strawberries novel") set in his Eastern Jewish homeland (he was born and grew up in Galicia, an Austrian 'Crown land', now divided between Poland, Ukraine, and Slovakia).

On January 30, 1933, all that changed. Hitler became Chancellor; that same day, Roth left Berlin, and never set foot in Germany again; soon to be instituted Nazi laws saw to it that he never earned anything from *The Radetzky March*; and a word was found for what had been and remained his wandering and short-run modus vivendi of hotels and trains and bars: exile. Thenceforth, his energies were divided between furious anti-Fascist articles — mainly read by other furious anti-Fascists — and a string of short, would-be potboilerish novels (*Tarabas* [1934], *The Hundred Days* [1935], *Confession of a Murderer* [1936]) read by nobody very much, which he wrote at an insane pace, and distributed among three, more or less unwilling, Dutch publishers, who always lost money on them, and were not always reconciled to the fact. It meant basically the end of anything resembling a literary career. Roth outdid Kafka: he was simultaneously strapped to *two* writing machines: one present and public and political, and one past and private and narrative-fantastical; one that depressed the writer, and offered challenge and confrontation, and one that — if everything went well — distracted the writer, and offered refuge and alleviation; one that was duty, and one that felt like dereliction; one that was urgent, and one that he merely needed for his survival; and each was antidote and poison to the other. Not surprisingly, in view of his drinking, his uncertain circumstances, financial troubles, a short temper, the hours he kept, and more "further complications" than one can shake a stick at, his health failed rather quickly. He died on May 27, 1939, not quite forty-five years old.

What is remarkable is that among the *disjecta* of those years, there are pages and passages and pieces ("Rest While Watching the Demolition" of 1938 is one sublime instance) and even whole books in which Roth forgot or transcended his atrocious circumstances, remembered what it was to keep faith with the reader, and managed to write at the top of his bent. The novels *The Emperor's Tomb* (1938) and *Weights and Measures* (1937) belong here, as do the novellas *The Legend of the Holy Drinker* (1939) and *The Leviathan* of 1934 or 1935, first published in excerpts in French translation, and not finally scheduled for German publication until 1940 by one of his Dutch publishers, by which time Roth was dead and the Germans had invaded Holland; the bound sheets were kept hidden, and the short book was published, "with a small delay," as the publisher coolly noted, in 1945. *The Leviathan* (*der Korallenhändler* was the original title, "The Coral-seller") is one of the pieces — along with the eponymous fragment *Strawberries* — salvaged from Roth's great projected Galician novel.

So much for the background to this particular little jewel. I offer as much detail as I do, because none of it — "of course" — makes itself felt in the novella itself. Roth, poor man, may have had the ghastly sense that the wheedle and distress of the begging letters he wrote during the days made themselves heard in the fiction he composed at night, but he was really far too professional a writer for that to be the case. Read the first six words — the classic "Russian" opening of a story of Gogol's, or Dostoyevsky's, or Chekhov's — "In the small town of Progrody," and you know you are in the hands of a very great master. At the same time, though, *The Leviathan* is not a fable pure, hermetically sealed from reality. It plays, for instance, sometime between "the war with Japan" of 1905, and the beginning of World War One. It is set at the edge of an empire, and on the cusp of an age, even though most of its personnel are innocent of both. It accommodates an outbreak of diphtheria, a coma, a run on a bank, emigration, the imputation of homosexuality (with "young Komrower"—or is that a shameful thought?), the modern sales techniques of Jenö Lakatos, the end of a marriage in sexual indifference and alcoholism and overwork, a false product, and a true death. All these things it has over and above its picturesque ethnological base, which one might dub "Chagall."

People don't often talk about tempo, and yet it strikes me as being a primary—perhaps *the* primary—quality in fiction, as much as psychological acuity, or style, or voice, or construction. What most strikes us about Roth may be his passages of full-throated, sumptuous description—of corals, of ships at port, of a summer evening—but there is also the brute and wonderful speed of change, with which a character arrives or takes his leave, or changes his mind: as Roth says, in this very story: "lightning is slow by comparison." This is what makes him, for all his avowed hatred of modernity and modernism (he had no use at all for tricksters like Joyce), modern and contemporary. Without that speed, he would be an inferior, hokey, and metronomic product. The pleasure Roth gives us, is, I would argue, entirely based on his absolute, minute, and uncanny control of the speed of his story. From control of speed come fluency and freedom, and comes this astounding and moving story that is so unlike any other, and that no one else could have written: not parable, not poem, not fairy-tale, not prayer, not farewell, but partaking of the nature of all five.

— MICHAEL HOFMANN

Joseph Roth

"The totality of Joseph Roth's work is no less than a *tragedie humaine* achieved in the techniques of modern fiction."
  —Nadine Gordimer

"There may be no modern writer more able to combine the novelistic and the poetic, to blend lusty, undamaged realism with sparkling powers of metaphor and simile."   —James Wood

"Roth's gifts are substantial, and of a kind rarer now than it was fifty years ago."   —*The New Yorker*

Joseph Roth (1894–1939) was an Austrian journalist and novelist. Born in East Galicia, Roth studied in Vienna before leaving school to fight in the First World War. After the defeat and collapse of the Austro-Hungarian Empire, Roth moved to Berlin, where he worked as a journalist. A moderate success as a novelist early on, he gained wide acclaim in 1932 with the publication of *The Radetzky March*, a look at life under the collapsing Empire. The rise of Hitler filled Roth with despair; sensing "great catastrophe," he committed suicide in 1939.

Michael Hofmann is an award-winning poet and the translator of such acclaimed authors as Franz Kafka, Ernst Jünger, Joseph Roth, and Thomas Bernhard. He currently teaches at the University of Florida.